My Butt is SO NOISY!

Dawn McMillan

Illustrated by **Ross Kinnaird**

Dover Publications, Inc.
Garden City, New York

My butt is so noisy.

My butt brings me shame.

It makes **weird** noises and I get the blame.

clicking and *ticking,*

humming and **strumming,**

clanging and banging,

I skip and I strut ...

as **extraordinary** sounds escape from my butt.

My butt behaves in a most
mischievous way.
Such bad manners when
folks come to stay.

They hear a phone **ringing**, and sweet sounds of singing. Then whistling and chirping and **burping** and slurping.

And ...

Popping and squeaking when Auntie is speaking!
Then a crash and a boom and …
Uncle leaves the room.

My cousins, though, four of them boys,
all want a butt that makes lots of **noise**.
And while they try hard it seems very strange
that each of their butts has a limited range.

Not a horn-blowing boat, not a musical note ...
No snorting, no snoring — my cousins are boring.
But ... my butt makes sounds **beyond belief!**

And ...

My cousins are failures, to Auntie's relief.

Poor Mom and Dad — what can they say about having a son who behaves in this way? They breathe and they sigh, but they hold their heads high.

And ...

Amid all the stares, the fuss and the tiz, they say,

"He's our boy and he's fine as he is."

But I need a new butt! A butt that is quiet.
A butt that is good and won't cause a riot.
A butt that doesn't go **honk** in the park.
A butt that won't scare the dogs with a **bark**.

No **slapping**, no clapping, no rapping or **zapping**.

No blipping, no **banging**, no clinking, no **clanging**.

But wait ...

Somebody is coming! Somebody is running ...
And then I hear ... so **loud** and so clear ...

"We've found him! He's perfect! Just what we need.
We'll sign him at once, when all is agreed!"

And now…

My butt's in the movies. I am SO proud.
My butt makes the noises, gentle and loud.
Just the right noises to go with the story …

Like...

BIG booming

explosions

to go with the glory.

All my hooting and hollering has quite a following.

I do **splishes** and splashes,

collisions and **crashes.**

Each cough and each sneeze.

All the wind in the trees, the sound of **tornadoes,**

the **swarming** of bees.

All the waves **rolling** in,
all the **thunder** and din.
Yes, my butt is the greatest.
And, here is the latest ...

My butt is famous! I'm known worldwide!
I have the **loudest**,
the **proudest** ...
the most **uproarious**,
Victorious ...

Sound-system
backside!

About the author

Hi, I'm Dawn McMillan. I'm from Waiomu, a small coastal village on the western side of the Coromandel Peninsula in New Zealand. I live with my husband Derek and our cat, Lola. I work from a small studio in my back garden, with a view of the sea. I write some sensible stories and lots of crazy stories. I had fun writing this latest crazy story and hope you have fun with it too.

About the illustrator

Hi. I'm Ross. I love to draw. When I'm not drawing, or being cross with my computer, I love most things involving the sea and nature. I also work from a little studio in my garden surrounded by birds and trees. I live in Auckland, New Zealand. I hope you like reading this book as much as I enjoyed illustrating it.

Bibliographical Note

My Butt is SO NOISY! is a new work, first published by Dover Publications, Inc., in 2021 by arrangement with Oratia Media Ltd., Auckland, New Zealand. The text has been altered slightly for the American audience.

International Standard Book Number

ISBN-13: 978-0-486-84731-3
ISBN-10: 0-486-84731-4

Manufactured in the United States by LSC Communications
84731401
www.doverpublications.com

2 4 6 8 10 9 7 5 3 1

2021